LOOK OUT FOR THE WHOLE SERIES!

THE CASE OF THE FISH
THAT FLEW THE COOP

Hodder
Children's
Books

A division of Hachette Children's Books

Special thanks to Lucy Courtenay and Artful Doodlers

Copyright © 2009 Chorion Rights Limited, a Chorion company

First published in Great Britain in 2009 by Hodder Children's Books

1

A Catalogue record for this book is available from the British Library

ISBN 978 0 340 98118 4

Typeset in Weiss by Avon DataSet Ltd,
Bidford on Avon, Warwickshire

Printed in Great Britain by
Clays Ltd, St Ives plc

The paper and board used in this paperback by Hodder Children's
Books are natural recyclable products made from wood grown in
sustainable forests. The manufacturing processes conform to the
environmental regulations of the country of origin.

Hodder Children's Books
a division of Hachette Children's Books
338 Euston Road, London NW1 3BH
An Hachette UK Company
www.hachette.co.uk

Chapter One

A gentle breeze wafted politely through the badminton net in Jo's garden. Badminton was that sort of game.

"It's nice to play a peaceful game for once," said Allie, limbering up on the far side of the net. Her blond hair bounced on her shoulders like glossy springs. "Nice, friendly badminton."

Max pushed his shaggy fringe out of his eyes and nodded. He'd learned from experience that it was always a good idea to agree with his American cousin whenever they were on the same team. Otherwise, he would live to regret it.

Allie smiled. "Service . . ."

Throwing the shuttlecock into the air, she hit it beautifully across the net to Jo, waiting on the other side. Jo made an athletic leap and batted it back. The shuttlecock floated back to Allie like thistledown.

Max couldn't help it. He yawned. "Are we all bored yet?" he asked.

"To tears," Jo agreed.

As a rule, the Famous Five didn't go in for gentle stuff.

"Right," said Allie, narrowing her eyes. "Unleash the hounds!"

Sitting on the sidelines, Jo's dog Timmy pricked up his ears as Allie cracked the shuttlecock as hard as she could. Jo slammed it back. Allie ducked as the shuttlecock whizzed like a bullet over her head. Max reached up and swiped it at Dylan, who was on Jo's side of the net. Somehow, Dylan threw himself sideways and returned it. Back and forth, back and forth blasted the shuttlecock. It wasn't badminton any more. It was war.

Finally, Jo fired the shuttlecock over Max and Allie's heads. It sailed out of the garden completely, and landed on a figure shuffling down the lane.

Sheepishly, the Five peered over the fence. Constantine Tarlev, the owner of the Falcongate crazy golf course, was wearing the shuttlecock like a tiny hat.

"Huhh," said Constantine in his thick East European accent as he took the shuttlecock off his head. "Shuttlecock only thing Constantine catch all weekend. Constantine sad."

Jo leaned her arms on the fence. "You said you were going to Bodwell Lake," she said with a frown.

"How could you not catch any fish? Bodwell Lake is *full* of fish."

Constantine shook his head. He looked like a tragic bloodhound. "No longer," he said. "No swimmy-fishies, no pretty ferns. Is wasteland."

"That's impossible!" said Max. Bodwell Lake was a well-known beauty spot a little way inland from Falcongate. "Unless aliens have been taking samples," he said after a moment. "You never know . . ."

Constantine's jowls flapped as he shook his head again. "Constantine's phone does not lie . . ." he said.

He held up his phone and scrolled through a pitiful collection of photos. A barren lake shore. An empty fishing hook.

"Constantine thinks fish must have been eaten by chompy-guy crocodile," Constantine continued.

The Five did a row of double-takes.

"England doesn't have crocodiles," Dylan said. "We have a lot of rain and cricket, but we don't have crocodiles."

Constantine thrust one finger in the air. "Is at least one," he insisted. "Constantine would have taken photo, but phone ran out of memory."

Jo took the phone and looked more closely.

"See? Is only sadness," said Constantine. "Constantine will fish no more forever."

Max peered at the pictures over Jo's shoulder. "Well, there's *something* very wrong at the lake," he said. "It should be a lot greener than that."

The others knew what was coming. They looked at Jo.

Whatever the problem was, Jo was reasonably certain that it wasn't a crocodile. "Let's go there," she said, passing back Constantine's phone. "*We'll* find out what's wrong."

It couldn't *really* be a crocodile.

Could it?

Chapter Two

The sun glimmered on the still waters of the Falcongate canal the following morning. Brightly painted boats chugged up and down, their pilots waving cheerily at each other.

Jo sat at the tiller of her mum's canal boat. Timmy sunned himself on the deck beside her.

"This canal takes us north of Mercerton," she called to the others. The waterway wound ahead of the boat like a sheet of shiny tin foil. "From there we moor the boat and hike to Bodwell Lake."

Allie crawled on her belly along the cabin roof towards Jo. She was holding a paintbrush covered in pink paint. "I need you to move," she told Jo, dropping down on to the deck. "It's time to paint the rudder."

Jo glanced behind her at the rudder. "I'm steering with it," she objected. "And why would you paint it pink?"

Allie beamed. "Because pink is the new red," she said, and waved the brush dangerously close to Jo's nose. "It makes the boat look happy."

Jo realised that somehow Allie had managed to paint the entire boat pink. She had highlighted it in a few places with little green and yellow flowers. A left-over tin of paint sat on the cabin roof.

"It makes it look like a giant baby's cradle," Jo growled.

"Well, the rudder has to match . . ." Allie pointed out, failing to notice the dangerous expression on her cousin's face. Getting down on her knees, she reached over the stern of the little boat and stretched down to where the top part of the rudder was sticking out of the water. "Can't quite reach the back though . . ."

She grasped the rudder and twisted it to get a better angle. This made the tiller turn abruptly. Jo was slammed into the rear door of the cabin. The impact jarred the tin of paint, which teetered on the edge of the boat's roof and tipped over.

"Woahhhh!" Jo spluttered, as a shower of pink poured all over her.

Timmy leaped out of the way just in time. He sniffed the paint warily.

"Oops," said Allie, straightening up. "Looks good, though . . ."

Jo wiped a dollop of pink goo off the end of her nose. Her expression had moved from dangerous to frightening.

"I'll go decorate the inside," said Allie, rather quickly. "Bye."

Before Jo could push her off the boat, Allie scampered through the cabin doors and disappeared.

Jo gritted her teeth and wiped herself clean. Then Dylan leaned over from where he was fishing on the cabin roof.

"I don't think this thing is ideal for fishing . . ." he said, waving at the boat.

As he did so, his fishing line flew out over the edge of the canal, and landed on the towpath.

"Whoa," said Dylan, noticing that his line had

gone taut. "Got something!"

He heaved and pulled at his line with excitement. A child's tricycle appeared from the undergrowth and landed in the canal with a sad plop.

"Nope," said Dylan, staring at the ripples. "Not good for fishing. Or speed – that tricycle can go faster than the boat."

"This is as fast as we're *allowed* to go," Jo pointed out. "Otherwise the wake of the boat would damage the canal walls."

A blond-haired figure coasted past in a kayak.

"That's why I'm on *HMS Max*," Max said, resting his paddle and grinning up at Jo and Dylan. He looked ahead. "Lock coming up – I'll open it."

Max pulled his kayak alongside the narrow boat as they entered the canal lock. Reaching up, he turned the lock-handle, opening the sluice gates. Water began pouring into the lock from the other side. Very slowly, the two boats started rising to the next level.

Beyond the lock was a tiny village huddled beside the bank of the canal. A small café and shop stood by the water's edge, together with a few outside tables. Woodland flanked the cute little waterside cottages, wrapping itself round the place like a dark green scarf.

Max tied the boats to the small dock.

"Next stop . . ." he said, glancing up at the canal-side village, "Mercerton."

Mercerton. It *sounded* harmless enough.

What could possibly go wrong in a place like this?

Chapter Three

Everyone got off the narrow boat and looked round.
It was a pretty place, with a few people strolling up
and down feeding ducks and eating picnics.

Holding his fishing rod, Dylan pointed to a snail
on the dock. "I recognize that snail," he announced.
"He left Falcongate the same time as we did."
Hunkering down, Dylan gazed at the snail's
waggling eye stalks. "Congratulations," he told it in
a solemn voice. "You beat us."

Jo was getting fed up with Dylan harping on
about how slow her mum's boat was. "Ha, ha, ha,"
she said sarcastically.

Dylan straightened up, smirking. Then he

11

tripped over his fishing rod and fell into the water. Jo started laughing for real.

"Woahhhhhhhh!" Dylan spluttered, trying to grab on to something that he could use to pull himself out of the freezing cold water.

"Jo – could you give me a hand?" he begged.

Jo obliged by giving Dylan a round of applause.

As the others fell about laughing, Jo noticed a dark-haired young man approaching them along the canal path. He stopped and stared at the bubble-gum coloured narrow boat. He looked a little nervous.

"That's a very pink boat," he said at last. "Pinker than most boats I've seen, it's safe to say."

"How about you?" said Dylan, turning hopefully to the newcomer. He was still treading water and trying not to think about how squelchy his trainers were going to be when he got out. "Could *you* help me out of here?"

The young man put one hand quickly to the small of his back. "Wish I could," he said regretfully, "but my back is bad." He rattled a little bottle of medicine at them. "I've just bought some headache pills for it."

Jo frowned. Something here didn't make sense.

"I'm Colm," said the young man brightly. "Where are you kids heading?"

"Up the Bodwell Lake trail," said Jo as Dylan finally scrambled out of the water.

"You can't!" Colm said sharply. Recovering, he added: "I mean, you shouldn't. I mean . . . there's a chemical spill up the canal a bit." He shook his head. "Ooh, nasty."

Dylan took off his trainers. They were even soggier than he'd expected. "The internet didn't say anything about a chemical spill," he said as he hopped about on the canal path.

"Oh, right," said Colm quickly. "That's a different canal. It's a *mudslide* on this one. That's what I was thinking of."

"Mudslide?" Jo repeated. "There are no big hills round here."

Colm was floundering. "Right – there aren't," he admitted, looking very uncomfortable. "But, uh . . . there are wolves. Oh, hungry wolves." He shook his head even harder. "Bad business, wolves."

The Kirrins looked at each other. This guy was *odd*.

13

"Do you feel OK?" Allie asked carefully.

Colm glanced up the towpath. A man was striding towards them, wearing long khaki shorts and carrying a rucksack. There was something frighteningly hearty about him.

"Actually, I don't," said Colm, and coughed weakly. "See? Not well at all. I think I'd better go and have a lie down . . ."

Backing away, he turned and scampered off into the woods that backed on to the canal.

"What's up with *him*?" said Max, staring into the woods.

Jo shrugged. "Who knows?" she said. "But two things are clear – he doesn't want us heading up the canal, and he's the worst liar since Pinocchio."

The hearty-looking man in shorts had now reached the Five's stretch of towpath. He looked Dylan up and down as he approached. "Heigh-ho, young man – do you need a towel?" he said in a chipper sort of way. "Some warm soup? We scoutmasters are always prepared. Charley Wilcox," he added, shaking hands with everyone. "My troop's camped nearby – I'm here to buy sunflower seeds. The kids snack on 'em. Healthy treats!"

Max brightened at the mention of food. "Speaking of healthy treats, who's up for a nice Scotch egg and chips?" he suggested. Realising this wasn't exactly a healthy treat, he added rather self-consciously: "And salad?"

"You guys go have lunch," said Allie, shooing her cousins towards the little café. "I've got a few finishing touches to make to the boat cabin."

An hour later, Jo, Dylan, Max and Timmy wandered back to their boat. Their stomachs were pleasantly full, and they'd almost forgotten about strange Colm and cheerful Charley Wilcox.

Jo threw open the double doors to the cabin. Allie glanced up from where she was plumping a cushion.

Jo staggered a little. "What have you done to my mum's boat?" she demanded.

Everyone goggled at the theme that Allie had got going in the little cabin. There was a hanging wicker chair shaped like an egg. Lava lamps blopped colourfully on the cabinets, and a moulded white alcove revealed a plastic dining table.

"This is a canal boat, not the *Good Ship Groovy*,"

said Jo, when she had recovered from the shock.

Allie looked crestfallen. "Did I overdo it?"

Dylan tried to sit in the hanging chair, which had caught his eye. It spun and rocked. As he tried to hang on, his arm got tangled up in the chain that attached it to the narrow boat's ceiling. The chair upended and tipped Dylan out.

"Wooaahhh – oophhhh," he said, sitting down on the shagpile rugs rather suddenly. "Owww," he added as the chair fell on him. "Maybe a little."

"I think this lamp is making me seasick," said Max woozily, gazing at the floating blobs in the biggest lava lamp.

Allie flapped her arms helplessly. "Well . . . Timmy likes his inflatable dog bed."

It was true. Timmy had settled down on a bright green inflatable cushion by the door and was in the process of turning round to make it more comfortable. After three turns, the cushion burst and sent Timmy flying as it deflated rudely.

"Rowfff!"

Everyone watched as the cushion looped and spun through the air. It settled, limp and flat, on Allie's head.

"Ew," said Allie from underneath the green plastic folds. "Maybe I could come up with a different design."

Dylan held up his hands. "No rainbows or unicorns, OK?" he said. "As a personal favour to me?"

Jo resolutely turned her back on the white plastic dining alcove. "Let's get up the canal and find out what that Colm doesn't want us to see," she said.

"Maybe it has to do with Bodwell Lake being de-fishified," Max suggested.

Everyone trooped up the steps and back on to the deck. Allie looked sadly over her shoulder at her groovy theme. Everything was going to have to change.

Ooh. Maybe that wasn't such a bad thing after all . . .

Chapter Four

The boat was making good progress towards Bodwell Lake. It was now painted white, with a sprinkling of blue snowflakes.

Allie stepped up to join Jo at the tiller. "We're in a Winter Wonderland!" she announced, waving airily at her creation. "How do you like the new theme?"

Jo concentrated on steering. It was trickier than usual, thanks to the inflatable fir trees decorating the deck. "How about a 'boat' theme?" she said. "The inflatable trees make it hard to see."

"I can fix that," Allie promised. She reached out and let some air out of the nearest tree. Its branches drooped until Jo had a clear view.

"Better," Jo said with a resigned nod. She squinted ahead. "Coming to a lock . . . !" she shouted.

"I've got it . . . !" Dylan shouted back.

The boat entered the lock and bobbed there gently as Dylan reached for the gate handle that would release the water and take them to the next level. But there was nothing there to grab.

"Hey, somebody's taken the gate handle!" he said in surprise. Riffing on this theme, he added: "The lock won't work 'cause a vandal took the handle."

"If we can't open the lock gate, we can't go any further," said Max. He was good at stating the obvious.

Timmy scampered to the bow of the boat. Peering towards the shore, he barked.

"What do you see, Timmy?" Jo said. She scrambled out of the boat and up on to the towpath. Bending down, she picked something up and twirled it between her fingers.

"It's a fluffy, white ball," she said in surprise.

Max clapped his hands to his face. "Oh, no," he said through his fingers. "A rabbit exploded!"

Jo tutted. Max could be a real idiot. "It's not a

rabbit tail – it's a ball of cotton wool," she said. Examining it more closely, she added: "There's a headache pill stuck to it."

"That guy Colm bought headache pills," said Allie, remembering.

"And he didn't want us coming up this way," Jo said with a nod. "I bet he's the one who took the handle."

Everyone stared at the thick reed bed at the edge of the canal. Something was rustling among the reeds.

"Hey – who's there?" Dylan demanded.

The rustling stopped.

"Ribbit," said an unconvincing frog. "Ribbit." As the Five listened, it changed abruptly to a bird call. "Caw . . . Caw . . ."

The Five looked at each other, unconvinced. They stepped off the boat and on to the shore. Quietly, they approached the reeds.

A dark-haired figure ran out, racing towards an even larger reed bed further along the canal shore. There was something in his hand.

"It's Colm!" said Jo, giving chase. "He's got the gate handle!"

The kids sprinted into the reeds after Colm. Their feet hit a squelchy marsh. As they splashed around in the shallow water, several frogs leaped out of their way. One fell down the back of Allie's shirt.

"Aaggh!" Allie screamed, freaking out and dancing on the spot. "Frog!" She started laughing helplessly. "Tickles . . ."

Timmy ran towards a long-legged heron, which had waded into the water ahead of them. Rather to the bird's surprise, Timmy dashed straight between its spindly legs.

"I found him!" Dylan shouted, catching sight of Colm up ahead. He put on a burst of speed – and disappeared into the reeds. After a moment, he emerged again. "Woooah!" he spluttered. "And I found the sinkhole we don't want to step in! This is where to stay away from!"

A duck flew in and settled happily on Dylan's head.

"And now there's a duck on my head, isn't there?" said Dylan, sounding resigned. "That's the third time this week."

Jo and Max were doing better. They had found a

narrow strip of dry land between the reeds, and had arrived at a wide stream. A log was bobbing helpfully in the middle of the water. They leaped on to the log, which sank very slightly beneath their weight and started spinning. Before long, Jo and Max were having to run extremely fast just to keep their balance on the log. The log won.

"Wooaaahh!"

Allie helped to pull Jo and Max out of the water. Dylan had got rid of the duck, but smelt of stagnant water. The others tried their best to keep their distance. Colm had disappeared.

"I saw him a second ago," Dylan said, wiping manky pondweed off his glasses. "How could he just disappear . . . ?"

In fact, Colm lay beneath a shallow stretch of water a couple of metres away. He held a reed between his lips, and breathed through it like a snorkel. When would these kids give up and go home?

The Five returned to the boat to dry off. The lock was still, well – locked.

"So, we're just stuck in this lock?" Max said.

"At least we have a nicely decorated boat to be stuck in . . ." Allie pointed out.

Jo was struck by an idea. She turned to her girly cousin. "Allie," she said, "you have some odd ideas about decorating, but they might turn out to be useful."

Ducking down into the cabin, Jo returned with a curtain rod. She took the curtains off. Then she unscrewed one of the finials, put the bare screw-top end of the curtain rod into the lock-gate handle and turned.

"Good thing I didn't go with shutters," said Allie, watching as Jo lifted the gate handle. Water poured out of the lock, bringing their boat neatly up to the next level.

Dylan rubbed his hands. "Bodwell Lake, here we come!" he cried.

Chapter Five

When at last they reached the lake, Dylan set up his fishing rod, determined to prove that he was a better fisherman than Constantine. Anyone could catch fish here. It was a well-known fact. They practically leaped out of the water and into your net for you.

After two hours, Dylan hadn't had a single bite.

"Bodwell Lake, you're letting me down," he said, peering into the water. "What happened to your fish?"

Jo and Allie were exploring the strangely barren shoreline.

"There were ferns growing here," said Jo,

examining rows of tiny green plant stumps. "All over. But someone cut them off at the roots. Why?"

Max had also been keen to prove Constantine wrong. Unlike Dylan, however, he'd kayaked into the middle of the lake to try his luck in the depths. Now he paddled ashore.

"This lake is completely fished out," he informed the others. He took off his kayaking goggles. "The only things in here are little guppies."

Jo sighed and stood up. "At least the small ones will grow up," she said. "Get the ecosystem back to normal. But how did it all get like this?" She waved at the broken, spoiled landscape around them.

Dylan was still stubbornly fishing. His fishing rod jerked and bent. He woke up with a start.

"Looks like there's at least one big fish left in here!" he said in excitement.

"Sorry," Max grinned. "Your line's snagged on the end of that log."

He pointed to something jutting out from the shore. Sure enough, Dylan's line was stuck at the far end of a log.

Dylan put the rod down. "You're right," he said,

and walked along the shoreline to the log. "I think I can get it unstuck . . ."

He stepped out on to the log, waving his arms for balance. But as he reached for his fishing line, the log twisted in the water.

For a log, it had the most enormous teeth.

"Whoa!" Dylan yelled, and fell into the water.

"Dylan!" screamed Jo and Allie.

It wasn't a log. It was the largest crocodile they'd ever seen.

Dylan swam frantically for the shore. The

crocodile lashed its armoured tail and chased him.

"Keep swimming, Dylan!" Max yelled, paddling his kayak between Dylan and the croc. "I'll head him off!"

The croc turned a beady eye on Max, opened its jaws and took a bite out of the front end of the kayak.

"Hey, I only rented this!" said Max, staring at the damage in dismay. "I'll lose my deposit!"

The kayak was sinking. With no other choice, Max jumped into the water with Dylan. Now they were *both* in the crocodile's sights.

Somehow they made it to shore. The croc snapped its jaws at Max's heels, nearly taking off the back of his trainers. Timmy darted out of the undergrowth and barked fiercely. Distracted, the croc turned its scaly head, giving the boys a few crucial extra seconds to climb a tree to safety. Allie and Jo were already there, perched on the branches.

Timmy was still barking. The crocodile swished its tail irritably. Feeling in her pocket, Jo pulled out a sandwich. "Hey, Smiley!" she shouted down the tree at the croc. "Fetch!"

Pulling back her arm, she threw the sandwich

into the lake. The crocodile waddled swiftly into the lake and gobbled it up. It then swam off into the distance and disappeared.

Feeling a bit shaky, the kids climbed down from the tree.

"Well! Hi-ho!" said Charley Wilcox, hiking down the shore towards them. "Doing a little bird-watching?"

"A little crocodile-watching, actually," said Dylan. He was still out of breath. "You're not going to believe this, but there's a fourteen-foot croc in the middle of that lake."

Charley Wilcox started. "What?!" he cried. "How is that *possible*?"

Jo shook her head. "We don't know, but it's there," she said.

Charley Wilcox looked nervously at the lake. "I'm here to check out campsites for my troop," he explained. "But if there really is a crocodile, I don't want them anywhere near here."

"My cell phone's charging back on our boat, but we can go to Mercerton and alert the authorities," Allie put in.

Wilcox snapped his fingers. "I saw a public

phone on that path about ten minutes walk from the canal," he said. "You could ring Mercerton from there."

Jo nodded. "That would be quicker," she said. "And you can go and warn your troop to stay away from here."

Charley Wilcox looked relieved. "Great," he said. "A few of them have mobile phones – we'll ring Mercerton too, just to be safe."

In a distant tree, Colm trained his binoculars on the conversation. As the Five shook hands with the scoutmaster, Colm continued watching. Very carefully.

"It would have been helpful if Wilcox had checked that public phone and seen that it hasn't worked in years," Dylan complained an hour later as the Five boarded their boat.

"That's true," Jo sighed. "The bird's nest built in the receiver would have tipped him off."

"Do you suppose Wilcox found his troop?" Max asked.

Dylan polished his glasses on his sleeve. "Let's hope so. Wouldn't want them at Bodwell

Lake. It's crocodile dinner time."

Allie's inflatable fir trees were still bobbing around on the deck.

"Allie," Jo called down into the cabin as she fought her way through the rubber trunks to the tiller. "I want your Winter Wonderland to melt.

Allie put her head out of the cabin door. "But I haven't put Mr Jolly Snowman up yet!" she objected.

The others groaned. Allie ducked back down into the cabin and scurried back to where a large, inflatable snowman stood grinning in the little dining alcove.

"Bwaaagghhh!" Allie cried as her foot went straight through the cabin floor and she plunged into the water beneath.

Dylan and Max dashed into the cabin. They saw Allie's head and arms sticking up out of the hole in the bottom of the boat.

"We're taking on water!" Max yelled. "Everybody, panic!"

Chapter Six

Dylan grabbed Allie's arms. Max helped to pull her up. As she emerged from the hole, more water gushed in.

Jo dashed into the cabin. She pulled a bicycle pump out of a storage locker, together with a length of garden hose. Fixing them expertly together, Jo stuck the end of the hosepipe out of the window and thrust the other end into the water. She began pumping.

"This won't hold it for long," she panted, as the water began to flow up the hosepipe and out of the boat. "We're already starting to list. We need a patch."

The boat was starting to lean dangerously.

"Mr Jolly Snowman started this trouble," said Allie, who had her feet firmly back on the deck. "*He* can help fix it." Grabbing the inflatable, she stuck it head first into the hole. It plugged the gap like a cork.

"There!" Allie dusted off her hands, looking pleased. "At least he was good for some—"

FWOOSH!

A geyser of water blasted the snowman up and out. It caught on a sharp coat hook and deflated. More water than ever roared up through the hole.

"I think we can still use him," said Max, and grabbed the snowman from where it hung limply on the hook. Laying it flat on the little alcove table, Max held out a hand to Allie.

"Scissors . . ." he said in a surgeon-like tone.

Wordlessly, Allie handed him her nail scissors. Max sliced the snowman up the front, laying the plastic wide open.

The boat was leaning even more. Dylan started to move some boxes to the side of the boat that was lifting into the air. Timmy hopped on to the boxes and settled down. The boat sank back very slightly.

"No – we want to list *more!*" Jo said. "Timmy, over here."

Looking puzzled, Timmy did as Jo told him. Jo, Dylan and Allie moved the boxes back, increasing the angle. The boat was now almost sideways to the canal, and the hole was out of the water.

Taking his patch of snowman plastic, Max scrambled over the side of the boat and placed the patch over the hole. He used some waterproof duct tape to fix it in place.

"OK – put her back down!" Dylan cried as Max stuck down the last piece of tape.

Jo, Allie and Timmy shoved the boxes back into the middle of the boat. The boat righted itself, and Max was plunged head first into the canal.

Dylan grabbed his cousin's legs and pulled Max back on board. "Sorry," he said cheerfully as Max got his breath back. "Should've pulled you out first."

Jo was down on her hands and knees, examining the hole in the deck.

"This is a very neat square," she said. "Somebody

sawed through it." She looked up at the others. "This was sabotage!" she announced.

By moving even more slowly than usual – to Dylan's surprise, this was possible – the Five coaxed the boat back to Mercerton. They found a dry lock and set to work, pulling the boat up on ropes so that Dylan, Max and Jo could fix a permanent patch to the damaged hull.

"Once we're patched up, we'll tell the authorities about the crocodile in the lake, and figure out what's going on there . . ." Jo told the others, wiping her hands on her long-suffering combats.

Down below, Allie had also been busy. Instead of icicles and snowflakes, the cabin now featured a selection of inflatable palm trees, a hammock, decorative fish-nets, starfish and cork floats.

"People didn't love the winter theme," Allie murmured to herself as she programmed her phone to play a steel-drum ring tone, "so – time to chill in the islands!"

Moving to the steel-drum music, she stood on tiptoe on a barrel and tried to hang a dried puffer fish from the ceiling. She lost her balance and fell into the hammock, which twirled like a dervish and dumped her on the floor. Still wrapped in the hammock, Allie rolled the length of the deck, knocking over two palm trees, a pile of coconuts and a lobster trap. She came to rest underneath the seating arrangements in the little dining alcove. Blinking, her eyes settled on something that *definitely* hadn't been there before.

After ten minutes of struggling, Allie got to her feet and hurried out of the cabin. "Look what I found!" she called to the others.

Max took the object from Allie and stared at it. "A heating pad," he said, turning it over. "The kind my grandmother uses on her sore knees."

Dylan looked puzzled. "What was someone doing with a heating pad?"

"When we met that Colm, he said he had a bad back," Jo said with a frown. "I bet it's his."

"So *he's* the one who cut the hole in the boat!" Dylan gasped.

Max shook his head sadly. "He *really* doesn't want us on this canal," he sighed. "But why?"

Allie remembered the first conversation they'd had with Colm. "Well, we know where he shops," she reminded the others. She took back the heating pad and weighed it in her hand. "Why don't we ask at the store who sold this to him?"

Chapter Seven

Mercerton's small corner shop was open. The Five gathered round the shop's owner, Mrs Wimple, who was cleaning one of the patio tables. The boat, which was canal-worthy again, stood by the dockside with Timmy keeping guard on the roof.

"Yes, I sold this," said Mrs Wimple, examining the heating pad. "Good little item. If you want one, I can order it," she said, scenting a sale. "Some chap bought all I had in stock."

"He bought them *all?*" Allie said, glancing at the others. "That's weird . . ."

"Can I interest you in something else?" said Mrs Wimple. She ushered the Five towards the shop front. "Got some fine spades," she coaxed. "Soap. Tea-towels. A clock shaped like Henry the Eighth. Bargain."

"We just want information about the man who bought the heating pads," Jo said firmly.

Looking disappointed, Mrs Wimple stopped ushering. "Some scoutmaster chap," she said at last. "Nice enough fellow. Bought lots of food. Even slightly 'off' pork luncheon-meat. I like a gent like that."

This wasn't the answer the Five had been expecting.

"Wait a minute — *Charley Wilcox* bought the heating pads?" Dylan checked.

"I'm going to take a wild guess," Allie said, grimacing. "He didn't call the authorities to report a crocodile in Bodwell Lake."

"Wilcox sent us on a wild goose chase so he could get to our boat and sabotage it," said Max, working it out. He frowned. "I don't think I like him any more."

"He obviously didn't want us coming back here to tell people about the crocodile," Jo guessed.

"But why would he lie to us?" Allie said. "And

where does Colm fit into all this?"

None of it made sense. Feeling confused, the Five headed back to the boat. Timmy stood up and wagged his tail in welcome.

"Come back any time!" called Mrs Wimple forlornly. "We're having a sale of snowshoes. Snowshoes and nutty fudge!"

Day passed into evening. Predictably, this was followed by night. In the gloom surrounding Bodwell Lake, something pale glimmered in the mud near the lake shore. It was a chicken carcass.

"Here, crocodile!" said Charley Wilcox in a sing-song voice from a safe position among the bushes. "Here's some lovely raw chicken ...! Yummy!"

He tossed out a second chicken. It landed with a squelchy *splat* in the mud beside the first. Then he crouched down and waited.

After a moment, the crocodile's nose peeped up out of the black water. It slithered up the bank and sniffed the chickens. Opening its toothy jaws, it chomped down and crunched into the first chicken with delight. Moving on to the second, it took its eyes off the bushes. Charley Wilcox and an accomplice seized their moment, tossed a large net over the beast and snagged it in one.

"Got you!" Wilcox shouted in triumph. In the net, the crocodile thrashed around in fury. "Tie his legs, let's get him out of here," he ordered, turning to his henchman.

Between them, the two villains managed to truss the crocodile and drag it away from the water. The creature was powerful, and it looked for a moment as if it might make it back to the lake after all. Wilcox and his crony hung on grimly. At last, the croc stopped fighting, and let them drag it away.

Silence descended on the fringes of the lake once again. Once he was sure the coast was clear, Colm emerged from his hiding place. Shouldering his backpack, he followed the scoutmaster into the woods. The expression of determination on his face made him look a bit like Jo. He was going to catch Wilcox red-handed, once and for all.

Chapter Eight

There were no crocodiles, scoutmasters or strangely nervous young men to be seen at Bodwell Lake the following day. The woods appeared to be empty. The only sound was the odd quack of a duck.

One of the bushes near the edge of the wood stood up. It hurried across a clearing from its previous spot near a large boulder. Then it settled down again at the base of a tree. Max's head popped out of the foliage, followed by his thumbs. He gave an all-clear signal.

A small fir tree, a rolling log and a tree stump all scampered across the clearing to join the

41

bush that was Max.

"This is making me very dizzy," said the rolling log. It sounded like Allie.

"At least your camouflage doesn't have ants in it," said the tree stump grumpily in Dylan's voice.

Timmy skipped out from behind a tree. Very slowly, the Kirrins peered out of their foliage disguises.

"We don't want Wilcox spotting us," said Jo, from the middle of the fir tree. "Now let's see if we can find him – or the crocodile."

The Five moved on, checking left and right. Timmy trotted beside Jo, resisting the urge to lift his leg on her tree trunk. His attention was caught by the half-eaten chicken carcass that still lay on the shoreline, and he whined with interest.

The tree, bush, log and stump all stopped.

"Look what Timmy's found," said Dylan gazing at the carcass. "Part of a chicken. I have a feeling the crocodile was here."

"He left the drumsticks," said Max in surprise. "They're the best part."

"A crocodile wouldn't leave any food," Jo said. "I think somebody grabbed him before he finished his dinner."

Allie stuck a hand out of her hollow log and pointed to a narrow trail through the mud near the shore. "Look at that track – the crocodile tail could have dragged through the mud," she said, sounding stricken. "Poor little guy."

The Five and their foliage followed the track in the mud.

"Tyres," Max said, staring at where the patterns in the mud suddenly changed. "I bet somebody caught the croc and loaded him into a lorry."

43

Jo pointed. "The tracks head into that valley," she said. "Let's go."

"Can we get out of our camouflage first?" Dylan begged as Jo hefted up her fir tree and prepared to run. "I don't want to get attacked by a woodpecker."

Everyone wriggled out of their disguises.

"Look," said Dylan, and pointed. "The tracks head straight towards those rocks."

Back in their normal clothes, the Five followed the tracks to a rocky outcropping at the edge of the lake. The tyre tracks made a small loop, then headed off along another route.

"It looks like they stopped here, then turned and went somewhere else," Jo observed.

The kids started examining the area, poking behind bushes and feeling along the rock face of the outcropping. Timmy sniffed enthusiastically.

Running her hands along the rock, Allie came to a spot which felt different. She knocked at the rock beside it. A solid *thud* came back at her. She knocked on the different spot. This time, she got a hollow *tock*.

"I think this rock has a door in it," she called.

The others dashed across.

"This is wood, painted to look like the rocks," said Jo, feeling the place that Allie had found.

Feeling for the edges of the door, the cousins pulled away a large panel of painted plywood. A cave entrance was revealed.

Cautiously, they ducked their heads and stepped into the gloom. They made their way down a short tunnel, which opened into a vast cavern with a mass of stalactites all over its roof.

The cavern held at least twenty cages. Shocked at what they saw, the Kirrins identified a mass of exotic creatures: a monitor lizard, eagles, hawks, parrots, a gorilla . . . and their friend, the Bodwell Lake crocodile.

"Wilcox is collecting endangered animals," Max whispered, dazed at the sight. "Now I *know* I don't like him any more."

"It's like a zoo in here," Dylan agreed, looking round.

Timmy sniffed at the cage of the monitor lizard. He leaped back, startled by the sudden appearance and dramatic length of the lizard's tongue.

"An *illegal* zoo," Jo added. "You're not allowed to own these animals."

"Well, someone's going to own them," said Max. He was studying a ledger he had found on top of a large stack of wooden crates. He leafed through it. "This book says where they're being sent. *Monitor lizard – Coventry. Bald eagle – Glasgow . . .*"

"Is Colm illegal to own?" Allie said, peering round the crates.

Jo looked confused at Allie's peculiar question. "Not that I know of," she said.

Allie beckoned her cousins. Everyone peeped round the crates – and goggled at the sight of Colm, bound and gagged and shut in the largest cage of all.

"Well," Allie said, "I think he's endangered!"

Chapter Nine

Checking that no one else was in the cave, the Five dashed across and set about freeing Colm from his cage. Colm made a gargling noise of thanks as they pulled the gag from his mouth.

"Where's Wilcox?" Jo demanded.

Colm rubbed his arms where the boys had pulled away his ropes. "He left," he gulped. "I don't know when he'll be back."

"What are *you* doing here?" Dylan asked.

"I'm a game warden," Colm explained, flexing his wrists. "I've been undercover, following Wilcox. Trying to find this place."

"But they found you first," Jo guessed.

Colm flushed. "I'm not very good at being undercover," he admitted.

Allie shook her head. "You're a very bad liar, that's for sure."

"But good at sabotaging canal locks," Max added.

"*Wilcox* sabotaged the lock," Colm corrected, "and took the handle. I found it hidden in the bushes. But I didn't want you kids to catch me and blow my cover."

They all heard footsteps echoing down the tunnel towards the cavern. Charley Wilcox's voice echoed towards them.

"All righty – who wants fish?"

The kids looked at each other in alarm. Wilcox must not find them here . . . Thinking quickly, Jo shoved Colm's gag back in.

"Aapphh . . ." mumbled Colm as the Five shut him back in his cage.

"We'll try to sneak out and get some help," Jo whispered, ramming the bolt home.

Colm managed to nod. Jo and the others scampered off to hide behind the crates again as Wilcox and his crony arrived in the cavern carrying buckets of food. The so-called scoutmaster dumped a bucket of small fish into the monitor lizard's cage.

"There you go, Ugly," he said, stepping back in distaste as the monitor lizard plunged its scaly head into the bucket. "I had to hike all the way to the river to net these. You've eaten everything in the lake."

"*That's* what happened to the lake," Dylan whispered to the others. "They harvested all the fish and plants to feed these animals."

"The croc must have gotten loose and hid in the lake until they caught him again," Allie guessed.

"It's a good thing this batch ships out tonight," Wilcox was saying to his henchman as he put armfuls of ferns into the other lizards' cages. "This area doesn't have anything left to feed them with." He flung a heating pad into a snake's cage. "There you are, Squirmy," he said as the snake lunged its head at him nastily. "It'll keep you warm during your journey."

"And *that's* what the heating pads are for," Max murmured, watching. "To keep the reptiles warm."

Wilcox had arrived at Colm's cage. He produced a sandwich, opened the cage and untied Colm. "And a sandwich for Mr Game Warden," he finished, taking out Colm's gag.

"Thanks," said Colm nervously. "I am hungry. And lonely. 'Cos there's no one else here."

The cousins winced. Timmy put his paws over his eyes. Colm was going to give them away!

"Of course there isn't," said Wilcox with a laugh. "Why would anyone be here?"

Sweat was now trickling down Colm's forehead. "Err, they wouldn't," he said quickly.

Wilcox was starting to look suspicious. "All right," he snapped, glancing around. "What's going on?"

The kids sensed some *serious* trouble.

"He's about to crack," Jo muttered. "We have to make a break for it."

They began sneaking quietly along behind the row of cages. They had to reach the exit, before ...

"Nothing's going on!" Colm squeaked at Wilcox. "I must have dreamed that someone was here. A mermaid, maybe. That's it – a mermaid!"

Wilcox grabbed Colm by the scruff of the neck.

"Oww!" wailed Colm.

Wilcox was now dragging him towards the gorilla's cage. "All right," he snarled, "you're going to tell me, or you're going in with the gorilla."

The gorilla stood up, growled and started pounding its chest.

"Kids!" Colm wailed in panic. "Run for it!"

The Five sprinted for the exit. As Timmy raced past the cage of a large macaw, the bird gave a loud squawk. Allie screamed.

"It's those kids!" Wilcox bawled, spinning round. "Grab 'em!"

Chapter Ten

Shoving Colm into the cage with the gorilla, Wilcox chased the Five. His henchman was close behind. The gorilla gave a roar at the sight of his new cage-mate. Unless the cousins could get him out of there, Colm was *toast*.

Allie was grabbed by Wilcox's henchman. Dylan shoved hard at a stack of crates, which fell on to another stack, and another. A huge domino effect was created, the end of which landed on the henchman and knocked him flat.

"Ooppphhh!"

Allie found that she was free again. She and Dylan sprinted to the gorilla cage, where the gorilla was circling Colm and bellowing.

"Being crushed to bits by a silverback gorilla is something you always think is going to happen to someone else . . ." Colm blubbered, backing up against the bars of the cage.

Wilcox had Max in his sights. He almost grabbed him, but at the last minute Max hopped up and over the monitor lizard's cage. Wilcox raced round to the other side, waiting to catch Max as he came down again. Meanwhile, Jo had opened the eagle's cage. The huge bird of prey flapped out and up to the roof of the cavern, where it circled hungrily.

Max decided not to climb down off the monitor lizard's cage, but up across another one instead. Grabbing a fish from a nearby feeding bucket, he turned and dropped it down the back of Charley Wilcox's shirt.

"Waahhhh!" squealed Wilcox, wriggling horribly. "It's going to take more than that to stop me!"

The eagle got tired of circling the rocky cavern roof. It screamed down at Wilcox instead, intent on getting the fish inside his shirt.

"Well," Max remarked as the eagle pecked and clawed at Wilcox, "that should do the trick."

"Get off!" screeched Wilcox, flailing his arms. "Leave me alone! Aaargh!"

The villain raced towards the eagle's empty cage. Shaking off the eagle at the last minute, he leaped into the cage and slammed it shut. Jo shot the bolt just as the eagle fluttered down to perch on top of the cage and glare at its trembling new occupant.

The gorilla had decided to hug Colm to death.

"Starting . . . to get . . . a bit . . . cramped," wheezed Colm, his eyes bulging at the strength of the gorilla's grip. "Ooh – left my car keys . . . in my trouser pocket. That's *really* . . . uncomfortable."

"Hey – ape man!" Dylan shouted, trying to distract the silverback. "Over here!"

He started beating his chest and hollering. The gorilla took no notice.

"I've got an idea," Allie panted. She pulled a stick of lip-balm from her rucksack. "C'mon," she coaxed, waving the balm at the enraged creature. "Banana-flavoured lip-balm – work your soothing magic . . ."

She reached into the cage and waved the lip-balm around, wafting its aroma towards the gorilla.

The beast sniffed energetically. Releasing Colm, it took the lip-balm from Allie and smelt it deeply.

"Thanks, kids," Colm said, sounding extremely relieved as Dylan released him from the cage. "That was close." He sniffed himself and shuddered. "Euchh, I smell of gorilla."

Max and Jo drag the semi-conscious henchman to Colm's empty cage and shut him inside.

"Hey!" said the henchman woozily, struggling upright as Max shot the bolt into place.

Jo put some ferns through the bars. "He can snack on that until the police get here," she grinned, and held up her free hand. It was time for some serious high-fives.

"Yeah, wahoo!" agreed Allie.

With their adventure at Bodwell Lake all tied up, the Five found themselves free to start enjoying their canal ride again. The sun shone obligingly as Jo steered along the glittering waterway, heading for Falcongate and home. Max, Dylan and Timmy all lounged on the deck beside her.

"Are we sure Colm can handle everything now?" Max said, stretching in contentment.

Jo steered gently round a family of ducklings. "He's a bad liar, but a good game warden," she said. "He says the animals will go to sanctuaries and Wilcox will go behind bars."

"I think that's what's called 'poetic justice'," Dylan commented, and linked his arms behind his head.

Jo grinned. "It's also called – 'Constantine can catch swimmy-fishies again'."

Her impression of the crazy-golf club owner was so accurate that Dylan almost fell off the boat.

Allie emerged from the cabin, wiping her hands on a painty rag.

"Well, finished," she said happily. "And I think I came up with the *perfect* decorating scheme."

Standing aside, she let the others admire the exotic birds and animals she had painted all over the roof, hull, sides and cabin of the boat.

"I call it 'Kirrins' Ark'," Allie finished proudly.

Jo nodded. "I think you finally got it right," she said, and smiled.

Epilogue

Jo pointed the videocamera at Dylan. He'd found a stuffed crocodile somewhere, which he had posed on a red wagon with a small go-cart engine attached to it. Max hovered in the background.

"Sticky Situation Number Two Hundred and Two," said Jo, by way of introduction. "You Have To Run From A Crocodile."

Dylan patted his stuffed friend. "Crocodiles catch their prey by using surprise – not speed," he informed the camera. "If you're confronted with a crocodile, run away in a straight line."

Max started waving his arms. "Aaagh – a crocodile!" he yelled, feigning terror.

Breaking into a run, he zoomed off between the trees. Dylan produced a remote control from his pocket and pressed it. His crocodile-wagon trundled after Max.

"Most crocs can't run much faster than fourteen kilometres per hour, and not for very long," Dylan continued. "Run in a straight line as fast as you can, and the odds are you will get away from a crocodile."

Max had reached a tree and was now rapidly climbing it. The crocodile-wagon ploughed straight into the tree trunk and broke into a hundred pieces. It was ruined.

Dylan winced. "Next time," he said bravely to the camera, "we'll tell you what to do if your mechanical crocodile needs repairing . . ."

THE CASE OF THE
FUDGIE FRY PIRATES

Read on for Chapter One
of the Famous 5's first Case File . . .

*Hodder
Children's
Books*

A division of Hachette Children's Books

Chapter One

A seven-metre sailboat sat on wooden supports outside the shed. Wearing grungy clothes, a toolbelt and a cap, Jo was in a suspended bosun's chair halfway up the boat's mast, polishing it with a cloth. Her elbow was starting to hurt.

"You've started, so you've got to finish," Jo told herself firmly, pushing her brown hair behind her ears.

She glanced down to where a large and very hairy dog was snoozing in the shade cast by the boat's hull. "You've got it right, Timmy," she sighed, wiping her forehead.

Timmy woofed gently and rolled on to his back.

"Be careful up there, Jo," warned Jo's mum George, who was potting something bushy in a terracotta tub down in the yard below. "If you fall, you'll crush my Devil's Moustache."

"Thanks for the concern, Mum," Jo said sarcastically. She turned back to the mast and rubbed it hard. "Shine!" she growled. "Shine more!"

She slapped the mast with her cloth in frustration. "Whoa!"

Jo's sudden movement made her chair wobble. She dropped her polishing cloth and flailed her arms as she and the chair went spinning head over heels, getting tangled in the boat's ropes.

Timmy leaped to his feet and started barking fiercely. Jo grabbed the mast and used it to spin herself back in the other direction. She did a neat backflip out of her bonds and landed on the ground like a gymnast, missing the Devil's Moustache by a whisker.

"I'll get this shipshape before Max and Allie and Dylan get here if it kills me," Jo said. She slapped the boat, which promptly toppled over on top of her. "Which it just might do," she added in a muffled voice.

The honk of a taxi horn floated down from a nearby hilltop.

"Oh!" said Jo in excitement. "They're coming!"

She struggled to push the boat off her as the taxi trundled into view, pursued by a tall blond boy on a mountain bike pedalling for all he was worth.

"Attaboy, Timmy," Jo said, scrambling free as Timmy tugged her arm. "Oh, I hope everyone's ready to have some cool adventures! I've got a lot of things planned."

Her jumper caught on the boat and unravelled. George raised her eyebrows.

"What?" said Jo. "I can have adventures with half a jumper."

"Whoo!" shouted Max, pedalling like fury behind the taxi. There was no way he was going to let Allie and Dylan get to Jo's house first.

Swerving off the road, Max plunged down the side of a hill, jumped a fence and started slaloming through some startled cows. "'Scuse me!" he shouted. "Pardon me, ladies! Short cut!"

The hill suddenly got steeper. Max twisted his wheels and took off, straight through the middle of a hay cart. Coughing and trailing haystalks, he landed on the other side and continued on his downward plunge.

The taxi containing his cousins was almost at Jo's gate. Putting on a fresh burst of speed, Max twisted his handlebars one more time and leaped over another fence, landing in Jo's yard just as the taxi pulled up.

"Hey, Jo!" Max called, squealing his bike to a halt. "It's so great to be here!"

His front tyre hit an upturned rake lying in the middle of the yard. The tyre exploded and the bike stopped abruptly, causing Max to fly over the handlebars towards the boat and hit his head on the ship's bell.

Dong!!

"That's going to sting a while," said Max, rubbing his head woozily. "Hey, great boat, though! Really brilliant!"

Dylan kicked open the taxi door. He was holding a DVD camera in one hand, his dark hair flopping to one side.

"Max, bash into that boat again," he said. "I can sell the footage to 'World's Wackiest Wipe-Outs'.

Do you think you could bleed a bit?" he added seriously. "That'd really help me out."

Allie scrambled out of the taxi. "Hey Jo!" she said happily, her blond hair bouncing on her shoulders and her pretty skirt somehow totally uncreased. "Love your half-a-sweater! What a neat style! Hi, Aunt George!"

"Lovely to see you, dears!" George smiled, waving her potted plant. "I'll go and get lunch ready."

Allie eyed the plant. "Is that some kind of . . . salad, Aunt George?"

THE CASE OF THE SNOW,
THE GLOW AND THE OH NO!

A division of Hachette Children's Books

**Special thanks to Lucy Courtenay
and Artful Doodlers**

Copyright © 2009 Chorion Rights Limited, a Chorion company

First published in Great Britain in 2009 by Hodder Children's Books

1

A Catalogue record for this book is available from the British Library

ISBN 978 0 340 98118 4

Typeset in Weiss by Avon DataSet Ltd,
Bidford on Avon, Warwickshire

Printed in Great Britain by
Clays Ltd, St Ives plc

The paper and board used in this paperback by Hodder Children's
Books are natural recyclable products made from wood grown in
sustainable forests. The manufacturing processes conform to the
environmental regulations of the country of origin.

Hodder Children's Books
a division of Hachette Children's Books
338 Euston Road, London NW1 3BH
An Hachette UK Company
www.hachette.co.uk

Chapter One

Snow lay like a fine white blanket over the mountains. Eagles soared overhead in the blue sky. It was a great day to start a skiing holiday in Scotland.

A bus trundled up the mountain and stopped outside an elegant little ski lodge called The Eagle's Peak. Five bundled-up figures stepped out. Four of them had skis slung across their shoulders. The other one carried a small suitcase in his mouth.

Allie pulled down the scarf covering her face. "It's pretty as a picture postcard," she said, gazing at the scenery. She shivered, before adding: "And cold as a meat locker."

The Kirrin cousins waved goodbye to the bus driver and trudged up the path to the lodge. Jo, dressed in her usual tomboy assortment of blue and grey and khaki, turned to Dylan as they reached the door.

"I have to hand it to you, Dylan," she said admiringly. "I don't know how you managed to get us discounted rooms at this place."

Dylan's glasses had fogged up in the cold. He took them off and polished them with a casual shrug. "Just the usual Dylan charm," he said. "Knowing what to say and how to say it."

As they entered the warm foyer, a short, round-bellied man stepped out from behind the smart reception desk and hurried over to them. "Ah!" he said in a cheerful voice. "Dylan and cousins!"

Jo smiled.

"You're late – as the sheep said to the fish pond," continued the man. "Your shift started an hour ago."

Jo's smile dropped away. As the man handed them a collection of mops, overalls, brooms and toilet plungers, everyone looked enquiringly at Dylan.

"What *did* you say to him," asked Jo, "and how *did* you say it?"

Dylan dumped his skis by the door. "I said, 'Mr Kwan, you're friends with my parents. Could my cousins and I get a discount if we work at your lodge?'" he explained.

The others gaped at him.

"We're *working* here?" Max checked, in shock.

"Lately the lodge has been doing about as well as a cactus with a tuxedo," explained Mr Kwan, handing Allie a large bottle of disinfectant.

"Um," said Allie, staring at the bottle, "is that good?"

Mr Kwan shook his head glumly. "It's bad. I've

3

been having trouble paying for staff. As the postage stamp said to the space shuttle."

"We're *working* here?" Max repeated, looking more confused than usual.

"Just a little," Mr Kwan said. He smiled. "Trust me – it'll be a *great* week!"

As he finished speaking, there was a loud rumble. The whole building shook. Everyone seized hold of something in order to stay upright.

"It's off to a shaky start . . ." said Allie, clinging on to a sofa.

Out on the mountain, the shaking continued. Large chunks of snow started to break loose, and an avalanche came thundering down the slope.

Chapter Two

Gradually, the rumbling slowed and stopped. Unperturbed, Mr Kwan led the Five into the employees' lounge behind the reception area. Lockers lined the walls, and a table and a mixture of chairs stood in the middle of the room.

"Huh," said Allie, her voice still sounding a bit shaky. She didn't even wince at the little room's mismatched chairs. "So that was an avalanche, right? In California we have earthquakes, but at least you don't get snow down the back of your shirt."

Mr Kwan nodded. "Fifth avalanche this week."

The cousins looked at each other, startled. Five

avalanches in one week?

"Isn't that rather unusual?" Jo asked the hotel owner.

"Very unusual," Mr Kwan agreed. "And bad for business. Like a milk-cow with a parachute, if you take my meaning."

They didn't.

Mr Kwan didn't seem to notice. "Let's get you kids started," he said, clapping his hands. "Dylan, you and Allie can help with the laundry and the dining room."

Dylan beamed. "Dining room, sweet!" he murmured. "I smell tips!"

Mr Kwan tilted his head and sniffed. "No," he said at last, "you probably smell the hedgehog meat we've been putting in the Irish stew."

Max turned green. "Remind me to eat at the tea-shop up the road," he whispered to Jo as Mr Kwan fussed round Allie and Dylan, making sure their overalls fitted.

"Jo, you can help out at the front desk," Mr Kwan said at last, satisfied that his new kitchen and laundry employees looked the part. "You look like you're friendly, good with people . . ."

Dylan snorted at this unfamiliar description of his cousin. In his experience, Jo was the opposite. Offended, Jo glared at him. It confirmed Dylan's instincts.

"Sorry," he said hurriedly. "Swallowed wrong."

Jo turned her back on him. Attaching a feather duster to her dog Timmy's tail, she gave him a dustpan to hold in his mouth and a brisk pat. Anything they could do, Timmy could do better.

"And, Max, you can be the bell-boy," Mr Kwan finished, handing over a smart uniform.

Max looked delighted. "I don't have to clean toilets!" he crowed, pulling faces at the others as he wriggled into his bell-boy's cap and coat. "It's better than my birthday!"

Mr Kwan ushered Jo and Max back through to the reception area. They waved cheerfully at Dylan and Allie, who turned and headed for the kitchen and laundry area with a sigh. Timmy wriggled out of his dustpan and brush ensemble and trotted into the reception area after Jo.

A tall, middle-aged woman with an outdoorsy glow and a lot of luggage was waiting at the front desk. She looked rather like a horse.

"My dear Kwan!" she called in a posh voice as she saw Mr Kwan with Jo and Max. "Simply bracing to be back at Eagle's Peak! It makes one want to tramp about!"

She started breathing deeply and marching on the spot, elbows pumping efficiently.

"Mrs Greensteeple visits us every month," Mr Kwan explained to Jo, nodding at the woman. "It's her respite from her duties in the Diplomatic Service."

"Before that, I was in the army," added Lydia Greensteeple, picking up her knees a little higher. "Got in the habit of marching!"

Jo gazed at her. She glanced down at the hotel register, which lay open on the reception desk. "Well," she said, "you can march right up to room one hundred and eleven."

As Timmy picked up Mrs Greensteeple's hat box, Max breezily tried to whisk up one of her suitcases. It didn't move. But Max did.

"Whew!" Max panted, almost losing his balance as he tugged on the suitcase. "Are you a travelling cement salesman?"

"Diplomat," said Lydia Greensteeple. "I travel

8

with books about countries I visit. Trinidad invented the steel drum! Makes me want to dance."

She broke into a mambo then and there, gyrating round the reception area. Jo and Max watched with open mouths. Mr Kwan didn't seem surprised. He'd seen it all before.

"There," said Lydia Greensteeple, coming to a brisk halt. "Invigorating." She glanced at Jo. "Young lady, if you could give me a wake-up call for seven a.m. tomorrow morning . . ." She turned and started mamboing towards the stairs. "Follow me, young man," she called over her shoulder to Max.

"Seven a.m.," Jo repeated politely as Max dragged the heavy suitcases along the floor and did his best to heave them up the stairs after Mrs Greensteeple. She picked up a clock from the desk to check the time. 12:00.

"Huh," said Jo in surprise, shaking the clock and then giving it a little tap. "This clock seems to think it's midnight."

It was still the afternoon. That was strange.

Chapter Three

Back in the kitchen, Dylan also had a look of surprise on his face as he stared at the controls on the dishwasher.

"This thing doesn't work," he complained to Allie. "Machines are supposed to do my work for me."

Allie was over at one of the washing machines. "Hmm," she said, "this thing keeps stopping too. "I guess we'll have to wash up by hand."

She and Dylan thought about this.

"It won't be *so* bad," Allie added hopefully.

Dylan had an idea. "Why would it be bad?" he said, sounding suspiciously cheerful. "I'm a

champion dishwasher. In fact, I bet I can wash more dishes than you."

Allie snorted and put her hands on her hips. "Yeah, right."

Dylan raised his eyebrows. "You don't think so?" he said.

It sounded like a challenge. Allie took up position at one of the sinks.

"Go . . . !" shouted Dylan.

At once, Allie started scrubbing dishes like a demon. Beside her, Dylan picked up a cup in a leisurely way, and gave it a little wipe. Then he yawned, stretched and ambled over to a chair.

Allie hadn't noticed. With her head down, she was flying through the washing-up. A stack of clean dishes was already teetering on the draining board. "I'm going to beat you, Dylan!" she said, sounding completely focused. "I'm beating you . . ."

She realised Dylan wasn't at the next-door sink. Looking round, she saw him in one of the chairs. His feet were up and his nose was in a comic.

Dylan glanced up to see Allie scowling at him. "Wow," he said in surprise. "I was wrong – you're much better than I am. I could only do one cup."

Allie stopped scowling. "Hey," she said, walking over to the chair and holding out her hand. "Let me see your comic a second . . ."

Without thinking, Dylan handed it to her.

It was a foolish move. Allie rolled up the comic and swatted Dylan sharply.

"Heyyy!" Dylan yelled, scrambling backwards to escape the blows.

"How 'bout a real competition?" Allie challenged, throwing the comic to one side. "To see who's the best worker for the week?"

Dylan looked unimpressed by the suggestion. "And I want to work harder than you because . . . ?"

"Because we let Mr Kwan decide who's the better worker," said Allie, folding her arms. "If I win, I get your laptop for a week."

Now Dylan looked intrigued. "Ooh – high stakes," he said thoughtfully. "All right – if *I* win, I get your phone for a week."

He stuck out his hand. Allie shook it. Staring each other in the eye, they both tried not to wince as they crushed one another's hands.

"I'm going to work harder than anyone's ever worked before," said Dylan in a steely voice.

A bell dinged somewhere over their heads.

Dylan dropped Allie's hand. "All right, shift's over," he said in his normal voice. "Let's go skiing!"

Jo and Max were done for the day as well. The Five needed no encouragement to whip off their work clothes and put on their ski suits. This was supposed to be a skiing holiday after all.

As the Five put on their skis near the top of the ski lift, Mrs Greensteeple strode past. She was bundled up for trekking, and singing and yodelling fit to start another avalanche.

"IT'S A LONG WAY TO TIPPERARY," she bellowed. *"IT'S A LONG WAY TO – YO-DUH-YO-DUH-LAY-HEE-HOO!"*

She waved at the Five. "Hello, youngsters!" she called without breaking her stride. "It's yodelling weather!"

"*I* say it's slalom weather," said Max, fixing the wristbands on his gloves once Mrs Greensteeple was out of earshot. "And we're going to have the slopes to ourselves."

The ski lift, which had been grinding down the mountain towards them, stopped with a metallic *thunk* several metres from the Five.

Jo threw her arms in the air. "So now the *lift* doesn't work?" she said. "The clocks don't work, the phones don't work . . ."

"None of the equipment in the laundry room will stay on . . ." Dylan added, agreeing with Jo for once. "What's *wrong* with this place?"

Mr Kwan came out of the lodge. Walking down the path towards the Five, he appeared to be carrying a desk lamp in his arms.

"Mr Kwan," Max asked as the hotel owner drew nearer, "do you know that everything round here is malfunctioning?"

"Do I know it?" said Mr Kwan. Lifting the lid on one of the dustbins that stood beside the ski lift, he threw the desk lamp inside. "Does the north wind make a salmon happy?"

"Uhh . . ." said Allie, at a bit of a loss.

Mr Kwan tucked the desk lamp's trailing flex into the bin and shut the lid. "Things have been conking out for a few months," he sighed. "The fuse boxes seem fine. I don't understand it."

"Maybe somebody's sabotaging your power source," Dylan suggested. "Have you annoyed anyone lately?"

Mr Kwan stood and thought. "I did have a run-in with Chester Pitt," he said at last. "He wanted me to hold a cross-country snowboard tournament."

The Five thought about this.

"Wouldn't cross-country snowboarding just be, ahh . . . standing in the snow?" Allie asked.

"Chester's very safety conscious," said Mr Kwan earnestly. "If he had his way, no one would ever do anything that was remotely fun."

Jo frowned. "Maybe he's sabotaging your hotel for revenge," she said. Her face took on a look of determination the others knew well. "Don't worry, Mr Kwan," she said fiercely. "We'll get to the bottom of this."

Chapter Four

Twenty minutes later, the kids and Timmy were trudging uphill, carrying their skis and wearing their helmets.

"How come to get to the bottom of this, we have to go to the top of *this*?" Dylan complained, gesturing at the mountain above them.

"Yeah," Allie mumbled through chattering teeth. "I'm turning blue, and it's *not* my colour."

She started some energetic jumping jacks to warm up her arms and legs.

"You don't need to do gymnastics Allie," Jo said, stopping. "I think we're here. This looks like the home of a safety freak . . ."

They all stared at the small cottage in front of them. Its front garden was decorated with dozens of 'do not' signs.

"No sledging," said Max, walking among the red-circled signs and reading them out. "No cycling. No running." He paused and stared at a sign near the cottage's front door. It showed someone with a book in their hands. "No *reading*?" he said, perplexed.

Dylan shrugged. "Hey – if you're not careful, you could get a paper-cut," he pointed out.

Jo was examining the small forest of milk bottles and the enormous pile of newspapers near the front door. "Either Chester Pitt hasn't been home for some time, or he really loves milk and current events," she told the others.

Timmy sniffed at the doormat and pawed it with a whine. Allie lifted the mat and withdrew a stack of post. "Hmmm," she said, flipping through them. "Lots of letters here from the county hospital. But wait – check this out!" She waved a catalogue at the others. "They're having a sale on cashmere!"

Jo wasn't interested in cashmere. She took one of the hospital envelopes from Allie and examined it. "Allie, could I use your phone?" she asked, holding out her hand.

Allie handed her phone over. Jo keyed in a number printed on the back of the envelope. "Hello, County Hospital?" she said after a minute. "Do you have a patient called Chester Pitt?"

There was a pause.

"Really?" said Jo with interest. "I see . . . thanks."

Hanging up, she gave Allie her phone back. "Chester Pitt was picketing the ski slopes a while

ago," she told the others. "He was trying to raise awareness about safety issues . . ."

The others pictured Chester Pitt protesting about safety in the middle of a busy ski slope. It didn't take much imagination to see where Jo was going with this.

". . . when he accidentally got hit by a bus," Jo finished, to everyone's surprise. They hadn't pictured any vehicles on the ski slope. "He's been in the hospital for six weeks. I suppose he should be safe there."

So. No Chester Pitt. The Five started hiking away from the cottage again, towards the ski slopes. They'd ground to a halt with this investigation already. It was depressing.

"Maybe somebody else is sabotaging the hotel," Allie began.

Dylan thumped his fist into his palm. "A crooked property developer is driving it out of business, so he can build a luxury resort hotel and make billions. Sweet!" he said enthusiastically.

The others frowned at him.

"Though, of course, wrong," Dylan added, looking a bit chastened.

BOOM.

They all whirled round. The distant sound was rumbling through the trees above them.

"Look what you've done, Dylan," Max said in disapproval as several more booms followed. "You've angered the Spirit of the Mountain." He raised his arms to the sky and intoned loudly: "Forgive him, Oh Snow Spirit – his greed exceeded his wisdom!"

Everyone listened. The booms subsided. Silence reigned across the slopes again.

"You see, I'm in with the Snow Spirit," said Max, looking pleased. "You've got to know how to talk to them."

Allie glanced over Max's shoulder. "Do you know how to talk to the Ski Patrol?" she asked.

A skier in a dark blue ski suit with an official insignia on it slowed to a halt beside them. He had a wind-reddened face and a sour expression.

"Yurnah mach hool!" he said.

The man sounded Scottish. But that was as far as Max got. "I don't even *understand* the Ski Patrol," he admitted.

"I understand him," said Jo, pushing forward.

"My great-aunt was Scottish, and she always talked with her mouth full."

"Arrna mo yuuh na hem!" said the man, waving his arms at them. "Hrrroo!"

"He says those booming sounds were dynamite blasts," Jo translated. "They set explosions to create avalanches in safe areas. This area's off-limits."

Dylan spoke slowly and carefully to the ski patroller. "Is it OK if we ski down from here?"

"Hwoo ma' kinna na oonla mair!" said the man earnestly. "Dunna och purrri ken eezel ruh wyruh? Oorn mo wheyan buh sneh mo hem, barr da yoosin na sheeeelrrr!"

Jo shrugged. "He says, 'Fine by me'."

Max loved a challenge. "Beat you to the bottom!" he shouted to the others, pushing himself out on to a smooth stretch of snow and zooming down. "Wahayyyyy!"

The others followed at once. There was no way Max was beating them back to the lodge. Watching them go, the Scottish ski patroller smiled. It made his face look sourer than ever.

* * *

The Five hurtled down the hill like arrows. They were all expert skiers. Timmy raced after them as fast as he could, barking wildly.

Allie looked back over her shoulder. "What is it, Timmy?" she said.

Timmy kept barking. Allie cupped her hands to shout at the others.

"I think he wants us to stop!"

Everyone shushed to a halt. Timmy pelted towards them, still barking. There was a low rumbling. The ground shook. Everyone saw the snowy caps on the mountain above them crack and begin to fall.

AVALANCHE!

"On second thoughts, I think he wants us to keep going," said Allie, pushing off again. "*Fast!*"

Everyone crouched over their skis to pick up speed. They jumped over obstacles in their path. The wall of falling snow was catching up.

"There's an avalanche shelter ahead – hurry!" Max yelled.

They sped towards the little concrete bunker in the slope. Taking off like birds, they flew through the air and landed just in front of the shelter.

Everyone dived for cover. And the roaring white devil crashed over everything and turned the whole world white.

Chapter Five

When the avalanche had passed, the slope was as smooth and blank and white as a piece of paper.

Somewhere in the middle of the piece of paper, Timmy burrowed out with his nose. Tail wagging, he started digging furiously with his paws. Gradually, the others emerged, spluttering snow out of their mouths.

"Between the malfunctioning equipment and the constant avalanching, I'm starting to think California has an edge over this place," Allie complained, pulling several lumps of melting snow out from the back of her neck.

Timmy sniffed at something that lay glittering in

the snow. Plucking it out of the whiteness, he handed it to Jo.

"It's a purse," said Jo in surprise, turning over the little brown leather object. "With quite a fancy coat-of-arms on it."

"Is there money in it?" Dylan asked at once. "Maybe there's a reward. If there's a reward, it's mine."

Jo turned the purse inside out. It was empty.

"No money. No reward," said Dylan in disappointment. "When's the next plane to California?"

"Hmm," said Jo as the Five gathered up their belongings and tramped down the rest of the slope towards the ski lodge. "These avalanches *and* Mr Kwan's stuff malfunctioning? All happening in the past few months?"

Dylan glanced at his cousin. "You think there's a connection?"

Allie raised her hands before Jo and Dylan could get into a discussion. "Uh, could we sort this out in front of a nice, warm fireplace?" she begged.

Mrs Greensteeple tramped smartly over the hill

in front of them. "Hi-ho, young persons!" she called, raising her arm and shifting her rucksack to a better position on her back. "I've been bird-spotting! Eagles! They flap, they soar . . ."

"I think I've spotted a cuckoo," said Dylan quietly, as Mrs Greensteeple began to demonstrate soaring eagles by flapping her arms and gliding in circles.

"You should be careful, Mrs Greensteeple," Allie advised. "There have been lots of avalanches lately."

Lydia Greensteeple flapped her arms more energetically. "Pish – they won't keep me from

tramping about," she said. "Look – there's a snow plough shoving it all away."

She pointed. A bulldozer was making its way towards them, digging snow as it went.

"Which reminds me," continued Mrs Greensteeple, "it's time for me to shove supper into my tum-tum. Bye-bye!"

"It's roast beef tonight!" Allie called as Mrs Greensteeple started off towards the lodge, still flapping her arms. "I'll serve you! I'm the best server!"

"No she's not!" Dylan shouted at once. "She'll drop it in your lap!"

Dylan and Allie's competition to be the best worker for the week was well and truly back on the road.

As Mrs Greensteeple walked past the bulldozer, its engine coughed and stopped. The driver climbed out of his seat and studied the engine, looking confused.

"Another malfunction," said Jo meaningfully. She glanced at the others. "I still say somebody's sabotaging this place . . ."

* * *

After supper, Allie and Dylan entered the laundry area. An enormous pile of freshly laundered, unfolded towels sat on a counter waiting for them.

"I'd say I was the superior server at supper," Dylan was saying smugly.

"You knocked a guest's toupée into his soup," Allie pointed out.

"He looked better bald," Dylan said with a shrug. He eyed the towels. "Come on – time for me to beat you at towel-folding."

Allie wasn't having that. She picked up half the stack of towels and staggered over to a separate counter in order to fold them up. "No way," she said, picking up the first towel and flapping the creases out energetically. "I am the towel-folding champion. One, two, three – *go!*"

Dylan casually carried his own stack of towels to a table beneath the room's ceiling fan. Pulling a bag from under the table, he removed four long, dangly springs. For some peculiar reason, the springs all wore gloves. Dylan hooked the gloveless ends of the springs on to each of the four ceiling-fan blades. Then he turned the fan on.

The fan rotated. So did the springs. Seizing the

towels with their gloved ends, they folded them expertly and knocked them into a basket that Dylan had carefully positioned alongside the table.

"Still folding towels by hand, Allie?" said Dylan, grinning. "How quaint. Maybe later you could churn some butter."

Allie tried to fold her towels faster. She started getting red-faced and dishevelled. It was *not* a look that she liked.

"Keep working," Dylan advised, as he got a carton of milk from the large fridge in the corner of the room. "I'm going to enjoy some nice milk in a comfy chair . . ."

He started towards a chair beside the counter. The lights suddenly flashed on and off, fizzled and went out.

"Waaaah!" Dylan yelled in the dark. There was a sloshing sound. "OK," he said after a pause. "I tripped over the comfy chair. And I have milk down my trousers."

"How quaint," Allie shot back.

Dylan struggled to his feet. He needed to get the milk out of his trousers pronto, or he'd end up stinking like old cheese. Crossing to the sink, he

felt his way around until his hand landed on the tap. He turned it on.

The whole room lit up in a faint green glow. It seemed to be coming from the sink.

"I'm not an expert on water," said Allie after a minute. "But I'm pretty sure it's not supposed to glow."

Dylan found a glass on the draining board. He filled it with the water and held it up. It glowed brightly. "I don't think this is sabotage," he said at last. "I think this is just . . . bizarre."

Chapter Six

It wasn't long before Jo, Max and Timmy had joined Allie and Dylan. Everyone put on safety masks and gloves. Until they knew what they were dealing with, it was better to be safe than sorry. Then they lit the room with a couple of battery-operated lanterns, and carefully studied the glass of glowing water. Timmy took a sniff and made a face. It *definitely* wasn't dog biscuits.

Over at the counter, Allie continued folding laundry into a basket as Jo held the glass up close to her face.

"It's a good colour for engine coolant," she said, turning it. "Not a good colour for water."

Max took the glass from Jo and carried it over to one of the lamps. The lamp sputtered and went out. When he moved away again, the lamp flickered and glowed once more.

"So whatever is in the water is causing everything to malfunction," Max concluded, pleased with the results of his experiment.

Allie looked up from her towels. "Well, keep it away from the TV tonight," she warned. "I don't want to miss *So You Think You Can Play Harmonica*."

As Jo took the water and tipped it down the sink, Dylan typed something into his laptop. He studied the results.

"There are three elements in Scotland that mess up electro-magnetic patterns," he told the others. "Only mailinium is found around here."

Max read the screen over Dylan's shoulder. "An unstable mineral, illegal to mine. Not harmful to people or animals."

"Used in refining oil," Jo added, peering more closely at the small print on the screen. "Produces dusty residue with green sparkles in it."

Allie gasped. "Hey, that ski patrol guy had green sparkles on his ski suit!"

The others looked at Allie in surprise. Allie shrugged coyly.

"I've always understood fashion," she explained. "Now I notice laundry details, too."

Max wasn't convinced. "Then why are you putting a red sock with a blue sock?" he said, eyeing the mismatched socks in Allie's hand.

Allie looked defensive. "Because . . . the guest in room two-one-two is a circus clown," she said. Matching the socks with their correct mates, she pulled a handkerchief from the pile and held it up so the others could see. "But take this handkerchief . . ." she said mysteriously, twirling the little piece of stiff white linen. "It has the same coat of arms as that purse we found on the mountain."

Max felt in his pocket and pulled out the little purse. Allie was right. The coat of arms matched perfectly.

"The handkerchief belongs to Mrs Greensteeple, so that must be her purse, too," Allie concluded triumphantly.

Dylan closed his laptop thoughtfully. "Maybe she has something to do with the avalanches," he said.

"Because she lost her purse where one happened?" Jo said, raising her eyebrows. "That doesn't prove anything."

Max sighed and put the purse back in his pocket. "Well, one thing I do know. She's a great tipper," he confided to the others. "I'll take this up to her room later. Ka-ching!"

Timmy pushed another basket of unsorted laundry to Allie with his nose. Giving him a pat of thanks, Allie took hold of a shirt. Several socks and towels stuck to her arm as she pulled it out of the basket.

"Hmm, forgot to use the static cling sheet . . ." Allie said, trying to shake off the items. But as she struggled, even more clothes attached themselves to her.

"Hang on a minute," said Jo thoughtfully as Allie tried to free herself from the clingy laundry. "Why would that ski patrol man have mailinium on him? Does he patrol near deposits of the stuff?"

"If he does, we should warn him," said Max.

The others made for the door. Allie fought on with the sheets and underwear plastered all over her. "Oh, heck," she said through a particularly

determined pillowcase that had stuck to her head. "Even clean laundry can be pretty tricky . . ."

When Allie had finally freed herself, the Five hurried out of the laundry room and outside into the snow. The air was bitter and fresh snow was beginning to fall.

Beside the ski lodge was a small building. It looked like an army barrack hut, and was decorated with a rope of colourful pennants. A stern, matron-like woman opened the door when Max knocked. She glared at them.

"This is the Ski Patrol barracks, yes?" Max checked. "Is there a dark-haired bloke with a thick Scottish accent here?"

The matronly woman pursed her lips. "That would be Hamish," she said reluctantly. "He's out."

Allie stepped forward. "Could we see one of his ski suits?" she asked. She gave her sweetest smile. "My cousins say it's royal blue, and I say it's teal, and I can't *sleep* till I know."

The woman looked unmoved. "Ski Patrol personnel only," she snapped. "You're not personnel." And she shut the door in their faces.

"Hey you lot!" Jo called from over by a window. "Come here!"

The others crunched across the snow. Through a window they could see a laundry room. Several worn ski suits lay in a basket. Bingo.

Max cracked his knuckles. "Who wants to come fishing with me?" he asked with a grin.

Chapter Seven

Within five minutes, Max had made a fishing rod by tying a hook from an old ski boot to the rope of pennants that had been strung across the front of the Ski Patrol building. He climbed on to the roof. Then he attached his line to a ski-pole and started lowering the hook through a skylight at his feet. With his feet up on the window sill, Timmy barked approvingly as the hook appeared inside the laundry room.

Carefully, Max hooked his fishing line on to one of the suits in the laundry basket. As he winched it back up, the line went taut.

"Feels like a whopper . . ." he grinned, and pulled

his catch up through the skylight. Then he slid down off the roof and triumphantly handed the ski suit over to Allie.

Allie read the label. "Hamish Macleod. Hand wash, line dry." She looked up. "Dylan, turn your torch on – see if it has green sparkles."

Dylan fiddled with the switch on his torch. It flashed, fizzled and went out.

"I'm counting that as a 'yes'," he said, scratching his head.

Jo frowned. "So we need to find this Hamish and ask him where he's been patrolling."

"Let's try the lodge," Max suggested. He dusted some snow off his shoulders. "There aren't many other places to go round here."

"And the lodge isn't freezing," Allie added, shivering. "Seriously – it's like I've frozen yoghurt in my veins."

The reception area in the lodge was warmer. But that was the only good news.

"No Hamish," said Jo, surveying the room.

Mr Kwan was at the front desk, reading a newspaper. As he reached for a bowl of nuts, he

accidentally knocked it to the ground. Nuts went everywhere.

"But an *excellent* opportunity to impress Mr Kwan," Dylan murmured.

He glanced at Allie. Allie glanced back.

"I'll clean that up, Mr Kwan!" Allie yelled, launching herself at the mess.

Dylan casually picked up the bellows that were sitting by the fireplace as Allie chased the nuts around the carpet and started picking them up one by one. He opened the bellows, sucking all the nuts up. Then he squeezed it shut. The nuts shot in a graceful arc across the room, where they landed in the wastepaper basket.

"Allie, Allie, Allie," said Dylan, shaking his head as he put the bellows back. "You use elbow-grease, I use *brain*-grease."

"We can check for Hamish in a minute," said Max, heading down the hall for the stairs. "I want to give Mrs Greensteeple her purse back first."

Dylan spun round. "Remember, I claimed the reward first," he warned. "I'm pretty sure that's legally binding."

The Five clattered up the stairs in search of room

one-eleven. The door was ajar. Max pushed it open.

Hamish was standing over Mrs Greensteeple's open suitcase, clutching a rucksack.

"Hey!" Jo shouted at once. "What are you doing?"

The Ski Patrol man snarled something Scottish at them. He rushed forward and shoved them aside.

"Hey . . ."

"What . . ."

"Woahhh!"

"He says it's none of our business," said Jo. "I vote we make it our business!"

Hamish was already halfway down the hall. The Five gave chase. Every time Hamish passed a wall light, it flickered and fizzled out. Finally, all the Five could see was Hamish's outline, silhouetted by the moon as he scrambled out of a window at the far end of the hall.

The Five climbed out of the window after him, jumping down into a snowdrift. Sliding down on their bottoms, they hit the ground running.

Hamish dashed towards a bob-sled that had been parked outside the lodge. He started downhill in a roar of smoke and snow. The Five sprinted to

another bob-sled nearby, and squeezed in. Timmy panted happily behind Max, who took the steering wheel. The others gave the bob-sled a running push, then hopped in and tucked themselves down. In no time, the bob-sled had picked up a huge amount of speed. Timmy stuck his nose out into the wind, taking bites out of the rushing air.

Hamish was a dot in the distance.

"Starboard!" Max yelled as they headed for a stand of trees.

Everyone leaned to the right. The sled steered neatly through the tree trunks.

"Port! . . ." he roared. "Port! . . . Starboard!"

Then suddenly there were no more trees. Instead, the side of a large barn loomed up in the moonlight. Max's eyes widened.

"Up!"

He steered the sled towards a nearby rock. Hitting it perfectly, the sled launched itself up and into the air. Sailing over the top of the barn, it landed on the far side of the roof and slid back down to the ground.

". . . and down!" Max roared, a little unnecessarily.

They were closing in on Hamish. The patrol man was now approaching a road, where a snow-blowing tractor was chugging along and blowing out a small blizzard. Hamish swerved in front of the tractor, straight across the road – and vanished from sight

There was no way they could get across the road before the snow-blower.

"And stop!" Max said reluctantly.

He turned the sled hard sideways and whooshed to a halt underneath the whirl of snow coming from the snow-blower.

"Wahh!" yelled the others. "Ooppphh . . . Aahhh!"

"Great," Allie moaned. "Hamish got away, and we parked underneath a blizzard."

Chapter Eight

At breakfast the next morning, Allie was
determined to beat Dylan at something. She was
already working at full pace, scrambling eggs and
frying sausages when Dylan ambled in. He was still
wearing his pyjamas and dressing-gown.

"Working hard?" he said. "Good girl. I'm in
charge of bread, right?"

Allie glared at him. Timmy took the opportunity
to steal one of the sausages she had just scooped out
on to a plate. Unmoved, Dylan took a loaf of bread
and set it on the counter. Pulling a metronome out
of his dressing-gown pocket, he took a pat of butter
and stuck it on the metronome's metal arm.

"*Allegro agitato* seems about the right tempo . . ." Dylan murmured, setting the tempo on the metronome. "Win-win-win-win . . ."

The metronome started clicking back and forth. Dylan held pieces of bread against the butter, quickly buttering it.

Jo and Max came in.

"We stopped by Mrs Greensteeple's room to warn her that Hamish was trying to rob her, but she'd already gone on her hike," Jo told them.

"Let's go and find her!" said Max, getting ready to stride back out of the door. "There's no time to lose!" He stopped and sniffed the air. "Ooh, what's that?" he asked with interest. "Sausages?"

Mrs Greensteeple was forgotten as Max pulled up a stool and started tucking in. Jo looked hard at him.

"What?" he mumbled, his mouth full. "I can't sleuth on an empty stomach!"

Jo said nothing. She just looked harder.

"OK," Max said, pushing his stool back reluctantly. "I'll take some with me . . ."

* * *

Dressed in ski suits, the Five pulled bandanas up over their faces to keep off the chill and followed a set of footprints through the snow.

"The tread is definitely from a hiking boot," said Jo, not taking her eyes off the trail as they came over a rise. "And we know Mrs Greensteeple hikes in this area."

"And she's the only person I know of who flaps like a bird when she hikes," Allie said, pointing.

In the distance, Mrs Greensteeple was stomping through the snow towards a clump of bushes, pumping her elbows as she went. Allie was right. She looked just like some strange bird of prey.

"I bet she's going into those bushes to build a nest," Dylan commented.

Someone else emerged from the bushes. The Five stiffened.

"No," said Max, "but she's flushed a weasel out."

It was Hamish.

The patrol man and Mrs Greensteeple had identical rucksacks. As the Five watched, they swapped them over.

"They *know* each other," Allie said, puzzled. She gasped. "He wasn't in her room last night to

steal . . . he was *dropping something off!*"

"Maybe some mailinium," said Jo. She thought it through. "I bet she had it in her rucksack the other day – that's what stopped the snow plough working."

"And she's a diplomat," Dylan put in. "She could smuggle the stuff anywhere. No one's allowed to search her suitcases."

"Which could be lined with lead," said Max. "*That's* why they're so heavy – to insulate the mailinium." He looked disappointed. "I'm giving her all her tips back," he muttered.

Dylan looked worried. "Imagine what would happen if mailinium got into the wrong hands," he said. "People could make *any* machine stop."

Max imagined water-skiing, sliding down a ramp in an undignified way as his tow-boat died. Dylan had a very different image, picturing himself with a broken vending machine that wouldn't give him back his money. And Allie screwed up her face in horror at the thought of her hairdryer fizzling out in the middle of a styling session. EEK!

Mrs Greensteeple was now shaking hands with Hamish and heading off. After a quick glance

46

left and right, Hamish disappeared back into the bushes.

"She's taking the valley route back to the lodge," said Jo, watching as Mrs Greensteeple strode off down the mountain, her arms pumping as usual. "But where did *he* go?"

There was only one way to find out. Climbing cautiously over the rise, the Five slipped and slithered down the snowy slope to the bushes. Dylan noticed something straight away.

"Hey, portable bushes," he said, picking up a bush and showing the others its wooden base. "Handy for camouflaging something . . ."

The others wasted no time in pulling the rest of the bushes away. Leading into the heart of the mountain, the gaping hole of a tunnel was revealed.

Chapter Eight

What are five amateur sleuths going to do, when faced with a tunnel? What would *you* do? Exactly.

The Five followed the tunnel. After a short distance, it opened into a wider cave. A small mining operation was in full swing, miners hacking at the cave walls with pick axes and others loading dynamite into a cart. Ducking for cover behind a stack of wooden crates, the cousins watched as Hamish approached the miners with the dynamite.

"Noot murrrnish gra froomuhn," he garbled.

The miners gave a sharp nod and pushed the cart down a branch tunnel.

"He said to take the dynamite and blast in the south tunnel," Jo translated for the others. "That's what's been causing the avalanches."

"And it's putting mailinium into the water supply," Dylan said grimly. "Allie, can you get some pictures with your phone?"

Allie held up her phone. "It won't work."

"Of course – the mailinium," Max guessed. "We're lucky we're not robots. We'd all be kaput."

Jo got to her feet. "Then let's just get back and tell the police about this," she said.

"Oh, dear," said a horsey voice behind her. "I don't think *that* would do . . ."

The Five spun round. Mrs Greensteeple had come up behind them.

"Oh, Hamish?" Lydia Greensteeple called. "Yodel-ay-hee-guess-who's-here . . . ?"

The Five exchanged alarmed looks as Hamish stumped over. He glared nastily at them.

Mrs Greensteeple raised her eyebrows. "I assume you can deal with these nosy-noodles?" she checked.

"Hwoomp, brrrrrdh-uh," Hamish growled in response, nodding.

"What did he say?" Allie checked with Jo out of the side of her mouth.

Jo shrugged. "Nothing," she said. "He burped."

Ten minutes later, five large barrels stood in the tunnel.

Hamish fastened the lids on the barrels containing Max, Dylan and Timmy. He checked the pile of dynamite stacked in the corner of the tunnel, and then turned to Jo and Allie. "Mooht whinna na hoohin brra . . ." he said, and laughed as he fixed down their barrel lids as well.

It wasn't encouraging.

"*That* wasn't a burp," said Allie after Hamish had stomped away and left them in the darkness.

"He's leaving us in this tunnel while they blast for mailinium," said Jo.

There was silence from Allie's barrel. "Well . . . stink," she said at last.

"*I* don't want to stick around for that," Jo agreed.

She started rocking her barrel back and forth. At last, it fell over. It rolled down the sloped floor of the tunnel and smashed into pieces as it crashed into the tunnel wall.

Jo kicked her way out. Getting up, she ran up to the rest of the barrels and started freeing the others. Timmy licked her face gratefully.

"Bring those barrel staves with us," said Max as everyone wriggled out. "We might need them . . ."

Back at the main cave, Hamish had finished unwinding the dynamite fuse which led back into the tunnel. He was so busy attaching it to the plunger that he didn't notice the Five sneaking up the mouth of the tunnel behind him.

"Allie!" hissed Dylan as Hamish went to press the

plunger. "Nail scissors!"

Allie whipped the tiny scissors from her pocket and snipped through the fuse just as Hamish pushed the plunger down. Nothing happened. Looking confused, Hamish glanced up – and saw the Kirrins grinning at him.

Before the crooked patrol man could react, the Five raced up to the cargo cart that had carried the dynamite into the tunnel. Kicking off the wheels, they dug out a length of rope from the bottom of the cart and quickly fixed the long, curved wooden staves from the barrels to the axles, to act as runners on their newly created sleigh. Then they pushed it out of the mouth of the tunnel, leaped aboard and started zooming down the mountain.

Chapter Nine

With a roar of fury, Hamish dashed out of the tunnel, putting on a pair of skis as fast as he could. He came after the Five like a rocket.

Drawing on their experience with the bob-sled, the Five leaned their weight to steer round a rocky outcropping. They were heading straight towards a steep snow bank. It was impossible to steer past it. So the Five closed their eyes and hoped for the best.

The barrel-stave runners cleaved through the snow, leaving a clear path before the speeding sleigh. Close behind them, Hamish launched himself up the snow bank like a ski-jumper and flew

through the air, angling his skis for maximum distance. He landed neatly alongside the Kirrins.

"You've got to hand it to him!" Max yelled to the others through the cold and shrieking wind. "For an environmental criminal, he's a very good skier."

The sleigh was picking up more speed. The Five leaned sharply to the right, steering well away from the Scotsman. They plunged on down the hill. Hamish was behind them again. Now they hit a frozen pond, skidding and spinning out on to the ice. The ice made ominous cracking sounds behind them.

"Woaaaaahhhh!"

Hamish hit the ice. He straddled the widening crack, somehow made it safely to the other side of the pond, and continued after them. Wondering if they were ever going to get rid of their pursuer, the Five leaned forward and concentrated all their efforts on building up speed. The ski lodge loomed into view beneath them as they caught side of Hamish bearing down on the back of the sleigh.

"Ahh, we're heading right for the lodge!" Allie screamed. "We have to steer around it!"

"No, we have to steer right into it!" Jo yelled, clutching Max. "And *duck!*"

The Five threw themselves to the bottom of the metal cart. It passed beneath the ski lodge's overhanging eaves and slammed sideways into the wall.

"Aaarghh!"

The snow on the ski lodge roof trembled at the impact. Then it started sliding off just as Hamish skied into view. A wave of heavy, white snow fell from the eaves and buried the Scotsman completely.

"Owwphhhhh!" Hamish yelled, before his head disappeared beneath the wave of snow. "Ummpph . . ."

The Five climbed shakily out of their sleigh and stood for a minute, catching their breath. Hamish struggled desperately, but wasn't getting very far.

"Well, well," Jo said, folding her arms. "Look who was on the receiving end of an avalanche."

Allie nudged her. "Look – we've still got Greensteeple to stop," she said, and pointed.

Lydia Greensteeple was standing beside a waiting car outside the lodge. Mr Kwan was

struggling to load her heavy suitcase into the back.

"And mailinium to stop her with," Max said, reaching into the bottom of the home-made sleigh and producing a chunk of rock. The others did the same.

Now Mrs Greensteeple was pulling away in a flurry of snow. The cousins gave chase. Taking their bandanas off their faces, they used them as slings to hurl chunks of mailinium at the car. Several pieces bounced on the road and slid beneath the chassis. The car's engine sputtered and died, leaving Lydia Greensteeple looking confused and dismayed.

Mrs Greensteeple flinched as Jo ran up and stuck her head through the window.

"The police are on their way," Jo told the cowering diplomat. Almost as an afterthought, she added: "And I'm cancelling your reservation for next month."

Chapter Ten

The Kirrins' eventful working holiday at The Eagle's Peak Lodge had regrettably come to an end.

Mr Kwan stood in the service area with Dylan and Allie. Jo, Max and Timmy watched from the sidelines. It was Decision Time. Who had worked the hardest – Dylan or Allie?

"Before you choose the Best Worker," Dylan began in his most persuasive voice, "check out my patented 'Dylan Dishwashing Device'."

He pointed proudly at the sink area. Mr Kwan's eyes widened. A conveyor belt was moving slowly along the work surface, powered at one end by a toy Ferris wheel. A spring-loaded cart was putting

dirty plates on the far end of the conveyor, and what looked like a backscratcher fastened to an old record turntable was pushing each plate along every time the turntable went full-circle. The conveyor belt trundled the dirty plates along to the running tap at the sink. At the sink, a mixer with a scrubbing brush instead of a mixing paddle worked at scrubbing the dirt away. Then the sparkling plates were being carried further along to a blow-dryer before one final shunt into a second spring-loaded serving cart.

Except that the serving cart was standing a few

feet further from the end of the conveyor belt than it was supposed to.

"Of course," Dylan said, wincing at the sound of smashing as the plates fell off the belt and broke into pieces on the floor, "the key to the 'Dylan Dishwashing Device' is putting the receiving cart in place."

Mr Kwan recovered. "I should think so," he said weakly. He turned to Allie. "Well then Allie," he told her, "as the hare said to the tortoise, 'You win'."

"Hey," said Max in surprise as Mr Kwan shook Allie's hand. "That one made sense."

Allie took Dylan's laptop with a flourish. "I think this is mine for a week," she announced as Dylan gaped at her. "I'm going to surf shopping websites and chat-rooms about cute boys and movie-stars!"

Dylan clutched his head. "No – you're going to infect it" he moaned. "It'll be a girlie-computer!"

"Or," Jo interrupted, "we could all just go skiing, like we came here for in the first place."

Dylan looked intensely relieved. "Come on, let's go," he begged the others.

"Great idea, Jo!" agreed Max.

"Wooah – can't wait!" Allie squealed.

"Race you to the ski lift!"

Allie handed the laptop back to Dylan, and the Five ran out of the door – leaving Dylan's Dishwashing Device to do its worst.

Epilogue

It was time for another Handy Hint.

Jo put the videocamera on her shoulder and put her eye to the lens. Dylan and Max were huddling round a small ice hut in the middle of a large, frozen pond. They had a fishing line, which they had dropped through a hole cut in the ice.

"Sticky Situation Number One Thousand and Four – You Have To Find Food In Freezing Weather," said Jo, by way of introduction. She tweaked the lens and waited.

"It's possible to fish through ice," said Dylan. His teeth were chattering. "Make sure the ice is at least eight centimetres thick – then it's safe to be on."

Max was also shivering. "Ice fishing can be really c-c-cold," he said. He waved at the ice hut. "It helps if you have a shelter."

Allie skated past the camera in a cute skating outfit. She gave Jo a twirl. In the background, Jo's parents Ravi and George came into view. They were clad from head to foot in ice-hockey gear, walloping hockey pucks to each other past a stretch of hoarding which declared: *Father Goose Ice Cream is pleased to sponsor Falcongate's Centre for Ice Excellence.*

"It also helps if you're not on an ice-skating rink," Dylan said a little grumpily. "That makes it hard to catch anything."

"Except a cold," Max agreed. "Aaaa . . . choo!"

Read the adventures of George and the
original Famous Five in

THE
FAMOUS FIVE'S
SURVIVAL GUIDE

Packed with useful information on surviving outdoors and solving mysteries, here is the one mystery that the Famous Five never managed to solve. See if you can follow the trail to discover the location of the priceless Royal Dragon of Siam.

The perfect book for all fans of mystery, adventure and the Famous Five!

ISBN 9780340970836